ITHDRAWN

Susan Laughs

D0785750
05464982

A Red Fox Book

Published by Random House Children's Books
61-63 Uxbridge Road, London W5 5SA,

A division of The Random House Group Ltd
Addresses for companies within The Random House Group Limited can
be found at :www.randomhouse.co.uk/offiices.htm

Text copyright © Jeanne Willis 1999
Illustrations copyright © Tony Ross 1999

9 10

First published in Great Britain by Andersen Press Ltd 1999

Red Fox edition 2001

This book is sold subject to the condition that it shall not, by way of trade or otherwise, be lent, resold, hired out, or otherwise
circulated without the publisher's prior consent in any form of binding or cover other than that in which it is published and
without a similar condition including this condition being imposed on the subsequent purchaser.

The rights of Jeanne Willis and Tony Ross to be identified as the author and illustrator of this work have been asserted by
them in accordance with the Copyright, Designs and Patents Act, 1988.

Printed in China

THE RANDOM HOUSE GROUP Limited Reg. No. 954009

www.**kids**at**random**house.co.uk

978 0 099 40756 0

Susan Laughs

Jeanne Willis and Tony Ross

RED FOX

Susan laughs,

Susan sings,

Susan flies,

Susan swings.

Susan's good, Susan's bad,

Susan's happy, Susan's sad.

Susan dances,

Susan rides,

Susan swims,

Susan hides.

Susan's shy,   Susan's loud,

Susan's angry,   Susan's proud.

Susan splashes,

Susan spins,

Susan waves,

Susan grins.

Susan's right,   Susan's wrong,

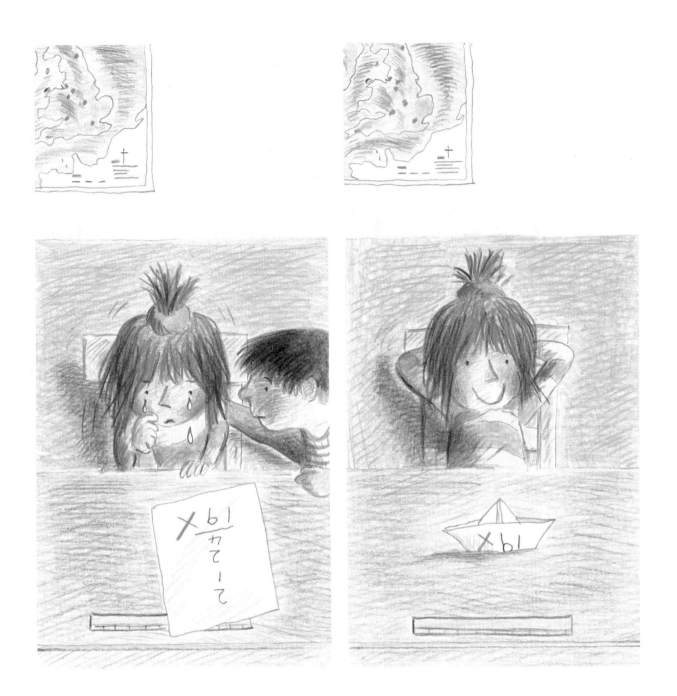

Susan's weak,   Susan's strong.

Susan trots,

Susan rows,

Susan paints,

Susan throws.

Susan feels, Susan fears,

Susan hugs, Susan hears.

That is Susan
through and through –
just like me, just like you.

More Red Fox picture books for you to enjoy:

ELMER
by David McKee 0099697203

MUMMY LAID AN EGG!
by Babette Cole 0099299119

THE RUNAWAY TRAIN
by Benedict Blathwayt 0099385716

DOGGER
by Shirley Hughes 009992790X

WHERE THE WILD THINGS ARE
by Maurice Sendak 0099408392

OLD BEAR
by Jane Hissey 0099265761

MISTER MAGNOLIA
by Quentin Blake 0099400421

ALFIE GETS IN FIRST
by Shirley Hughes 0099256053

OI! GET OFF OUR TRAIN
by John Burningham 009985340X

PERTH AND KINROSS LIBRARIES